W9-CFQ-451

HAN SOLO: VOLUME 1

It is a period of unrest. In a galaxy oppressed by the Empire's unrelenting brutality, there is little hope for change. Nonetheless, rebels have banded together to fight back against such corruption.

While the Rebellion grows in power, Imperials fight to crush any hope for an overthrow. With the Empire's hands full, the opportunities for crime are endless.

HAN SOLO has taken a step back from the rebel cause, returning his focus to what he does best - smuggling. Untrusting by nature, he's skeptical of any who cross his path. Unfortunately for him, he cannot stay under the radar forever....

MARJORIE LIU
Writer

MARK BROOKS
Artist

SONIA OBACK
Colors

LEE BERMEJO
Cover Artist

VC's JOE CARAMAGNA
Letterer

HEATHER ANTOS
Assistant Editor

JORDAN D. WHITE
Editor

C.B. CEBULSKI
Executive Editor

AXEL ALONSO
Editor In Chief

JOE QUESADA
Chief Creative Officer

DAN BUCKLEY
Publisher

For Lucasfilm:
Creative Director MICHAEL SIGLAIN
Senior Editor FRANK PARISI
Lucasfilm Story Group RAYNE ROBERTS, PABLO HIDALGO, LELAND CHEE, MATT MARTIN

ABDO
Spotlight

ABDOPUBLISHING.COM

Reinforced library bound edition published in 2018 by Spotlight,
a division of ABDO, PO Box 398166, Minneapolis, Minnesota 55439.
Spotlight produces high-quality reinforced library bound editions for
schools and libraries. Published by agreement with Marvel Characters, Inc.

Printed in the United States of America, North Mankato, Minnesota.
042017
092017

THIS BOOK CONTAINS
RECYCLED MATERIALS

marvelkids.com

STAR WARS © & TM 2017 LUCASFILM LTD.

PUBLISHER'S CATALOGING IN PUBLICATION DATA

Names: Liu, Marjorie, author. | Brooks, Mark ; Oback, Sonia ; Milla, Matt,
   illustrators.
Title: Han Solo / writer: Marjorie Liu ; art: Mark Brooks ; Sonia Oback ; Matt Milla.
Description: Reinforced library bound edition. | Minneapolis, Minnesota : Spotlight,
   2018. | Series: Star wars : Han Solo | Volumes 1, 2, 3, and 5 written by Marjorie
   Liu ; illustrated by Mark Brooks, & Sonia Oback. | Volume 4 written by Marjorie
   Liu ; illustrated by Mark Brooks, Sonia Oback, & Matt Milla.
Summary: When Princess Leia approaches him with an offer too good to refuse,
   Han Solo finds himself flying in one of the galaxy's most dangerous races, the
   Dragon Void, as a cover to find a mysterious rebel spy who may have turned
   traitor.
Identifiers: LCCN 2017931205 | ISBN 9781532140150 (volume 1) | ISBN
   9781532140167 (volume 2) | ISBN 9781532140174 (volume 3) | ISBN
   9781532140181 (volume 4) | ISBN 9781532140198 (volume 5)
Subjects: LCSH: Solo, Han (Fictitious character)--Juvenile fiction. | Space warfare--
   Juvenile fiction. | Adventure and adventurers--Juvenile fiction. | Comic book,
   strips, etc.--Juvenile fiction. | Graphic novels--Juvenile fiction.
Classification: DDC 741.5--dc23
LC record available at https://lccn.loc.gov/2017931205

Spotlight
A Division of ABDO
abdopublishing.com

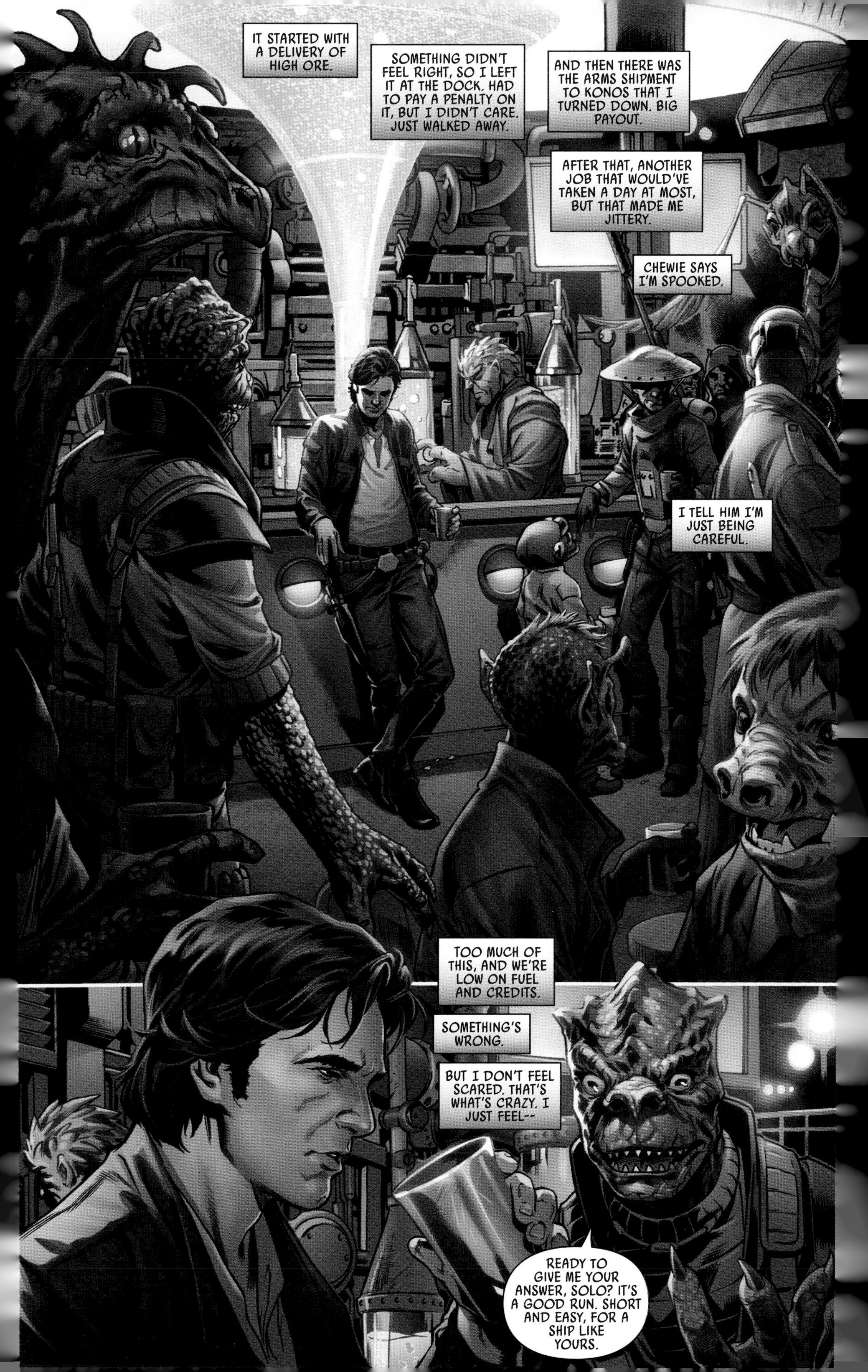
IT STARTED WITH A DELIVERY OF HIGH ORE.
SOMETHING DIDN'T FEEL RIGHT, SO I LEFT IT AT THE DOCK. HAD TO PAY A PENALTY ON IT, BUT I DIDN'T CARE. JUST WALKED AWAY.
AND THEN THERE WAS THE ARMS SHIPMENT TO KONOS THAT I TURNED DOWN. BIG PAYOUT.
AFTER THAT, ANOTHER JOB THAT WOULD'VE TAKEN A DAY AT MOST, BUT THAT MADE ME JITTERY.
CHEWIE SAYS I'M SPOOKED.
I TELL HIM I'M JUST BEING CAREFUL.
TOO MUCH OF THIS, AND WE'RE LOW ON FUEL AND CREDITS.
SOMETHING'S WRONG.
BUT I DON'T FEEL SCARED. THAT'S WHAT'S CRAZY. I JUST FEEL--
READY TO GIVE ME YOUR ANSWER, SOLO? IT'S A GOOD RUN. SHORT AND EASY, FOR A SHIP LIKE YOURS.

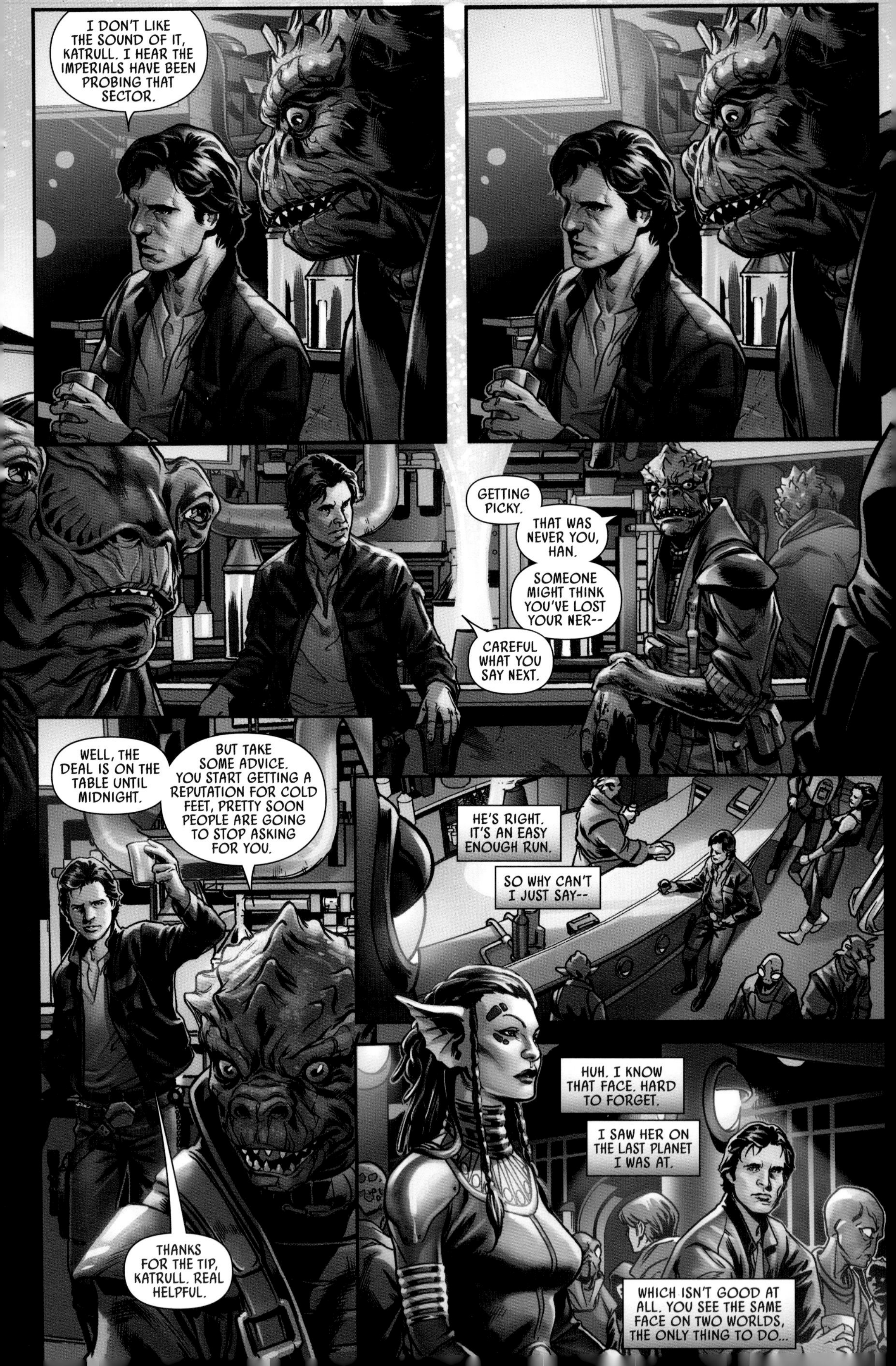
I DON'T LIKE THE SOUND OF IT, KATRULL. I HEAR THE IMPERIALS HAVE BEEN PROBING THAT SECTOR.
GETTING PICKY.
THAT WAS NEVER YOU, HAN.
SOMEONE MIGHT THINK YOU'VE LOST YOUR NER--
CAREFUL WHAT YOU SAY NEXT.
WELL, THE DEAL IS ON THE TABLE UNTIL MIDNIGHT.
BUT TAKE SOME ADVICE. YOU START GETTING A REPUTATION FOR COLD FEET, PRETTY SOON PEOPLE ARE GOING TO STOP ASKING FOR YOU.
THANKS FOR THE TIP, KATRULL. REAL HELPFUL.
HE'S RIGHT. IT'S AN EASY ENOUGH RUN.
SO WHY CAN'T I JUST SAY--
HUH. I KNOW THAT FACE. HARD TO FORGET.
I SAW HER ON THE LAST PLANET I WAS AT.
WHICH ISN'T GOOD AT ALL. YOU SEE THE SAME FACE ON TWO WORLDS, THE ONLY THING TO DO...

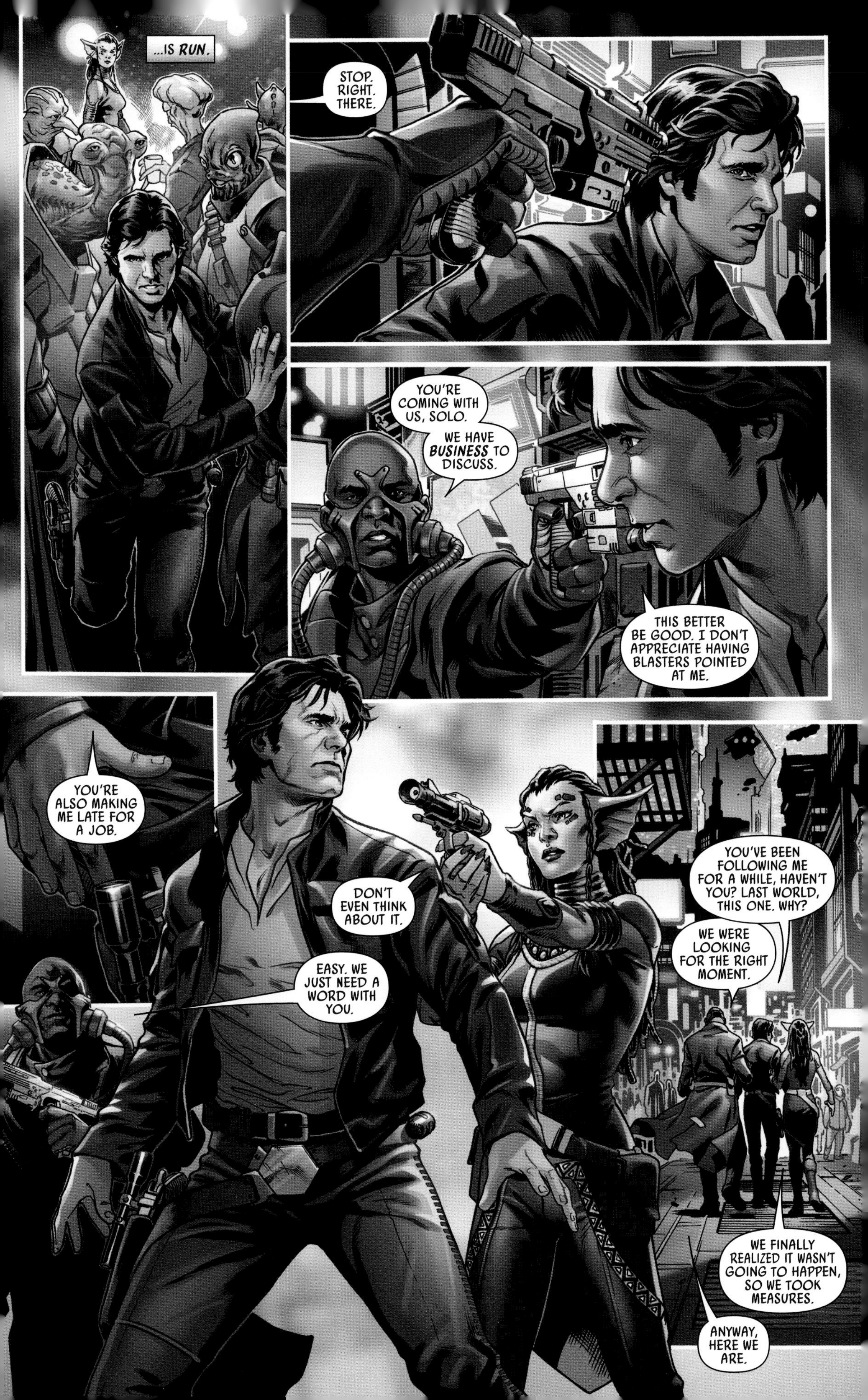
...IS RUN.
STOP. RIGHT. THERE.
YOU'RE COMING WITH US, SOLO.
WE HAVE BUSINESS TO DISCUSS.
THIS BETTER BE GOOD. I DON'T APPRECIATE HAVING BLASTERS POINTED AT ME.
YOU'RE ALSO MAKING ME LATE FOR A JOB.
DON'T EVEN THINK ABOUT IT.
EASY. WE JUST NEED A WORD WITH YOU.
YOU'VE BEEN FOLLOWING ME FOR A WHILE, HAVEN'T YOU? LAST WORLD, THIS ONE. WHY?
WE WERE LOOKING FOR THE RIGHT MOMENT.
WE FINALLY REALIZED IT WASN'T GOING TO HAPPEN, SO WE TOOK MEASURES.
ANYWAY, HERE WE ARE.

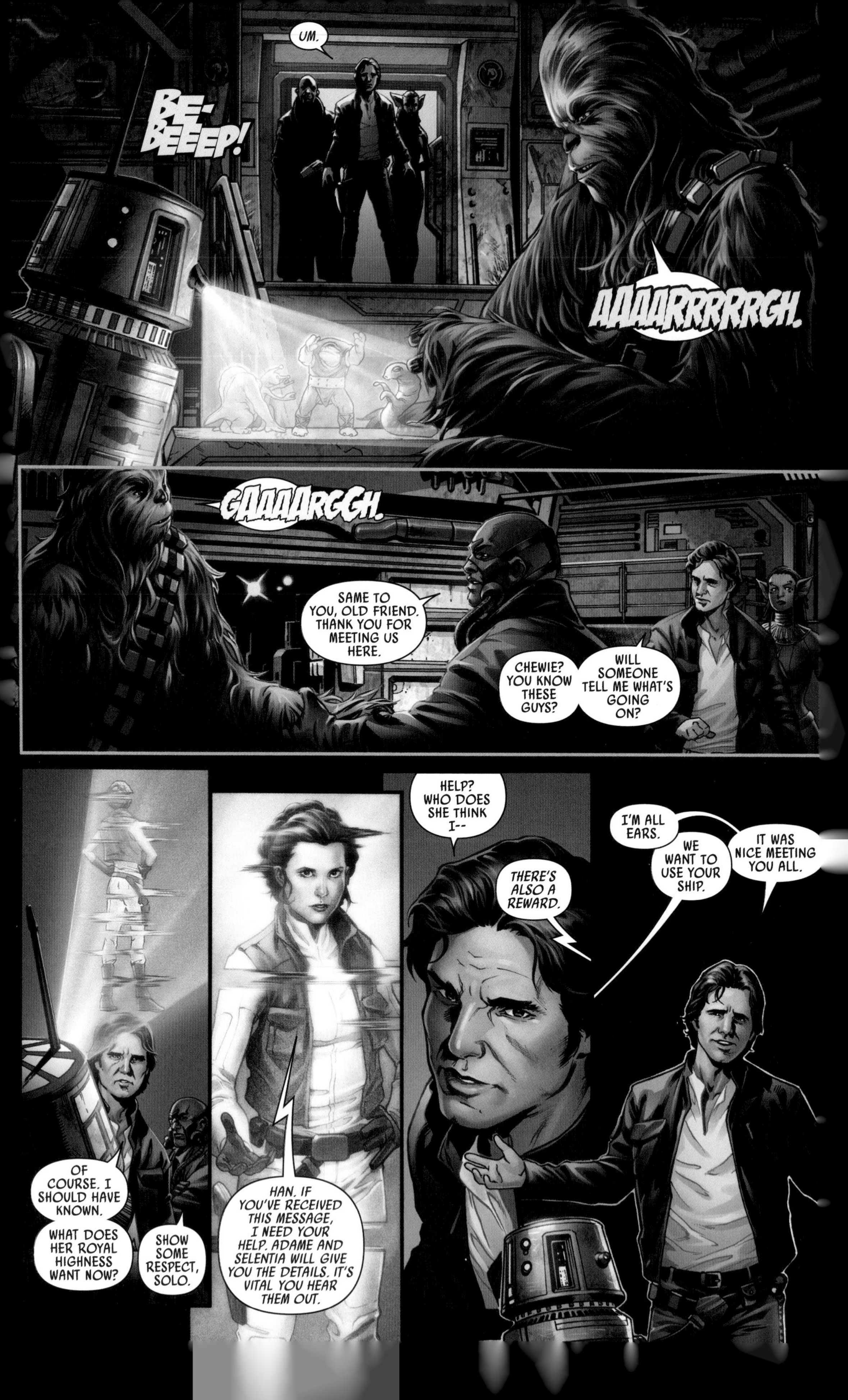

UM.
BE-BEEEP!
AAAARRRRRGH.
GAAAARGGH.
SAME TO YOU, OLD FRIEND. THANK YOU FOR MEETING US HERE.
CHEWIE? YOU KNOW THESE GUYS?
WILL SOMEONE TELL ME WHAT'S GOING ON?
OF COURSE. I SHOULD HAVE KNOWN.
WHAT DOES HER ROYAL HIGHNESS WANT NOW?
SHOW SOME RESPECT, SOLO.
HAN, IF YOU'VE RECEIVED THIS MESSAGE, I NEED YOUR HELP. ADAME AND SELENTIA WILL GIVE YOU THE DETAILS. IT'S VITAL YOU HEAR THEM OUT.
HELP? WHO DOES SHE THINK I--
THERE'S ALSO A REWARD.
I'M ALL EARS.
WE WANT TO USE YOUR SHIP.
IT WAS NICE MEETING YOU ALL.

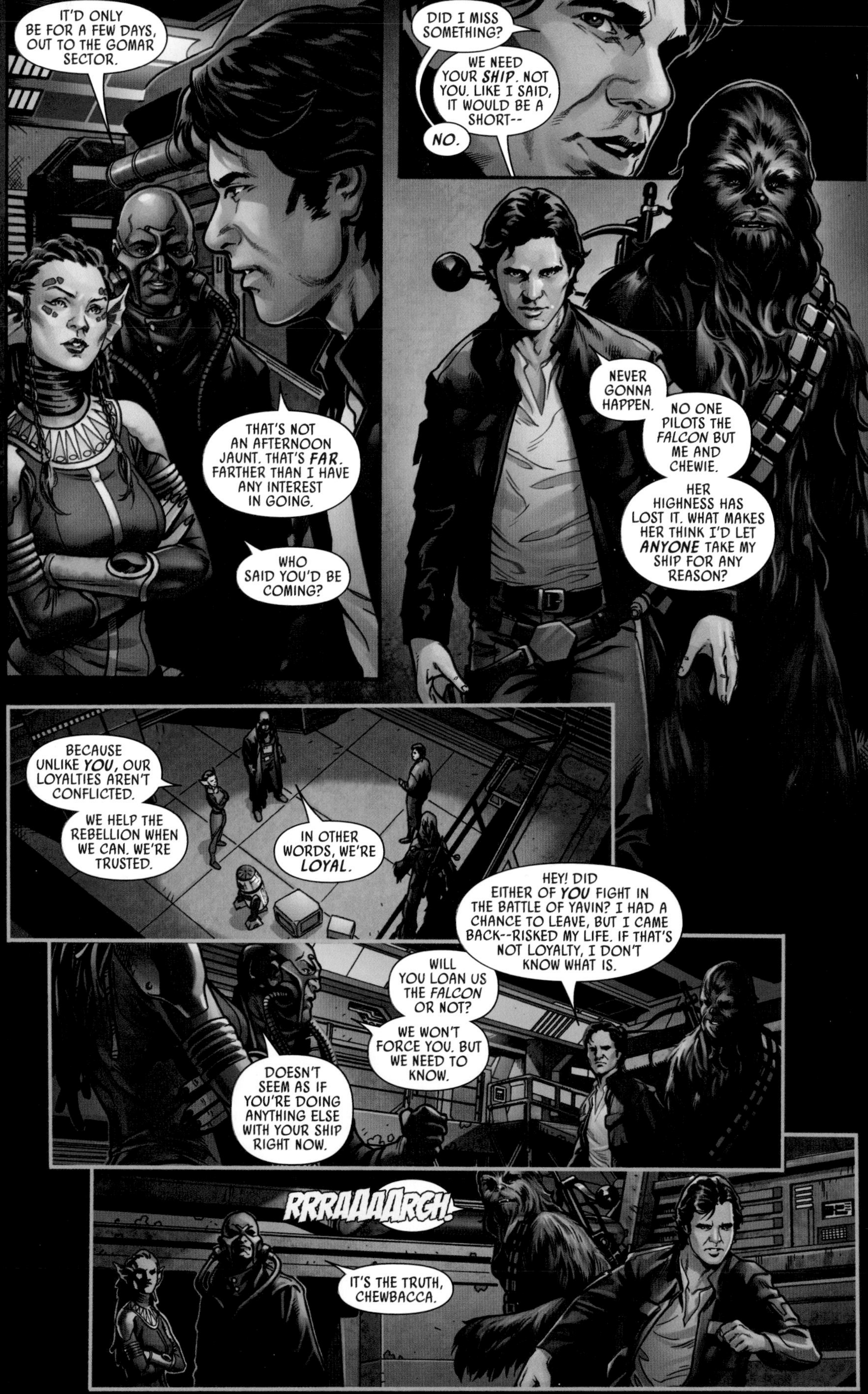
IT'D ONLY BE FOR A FEW DAYS, OUT TO THE GOMAR SECTOR.
THAT'S NOT AN AFTERNOON JAUNT. THAT'S FAR. FARTHER THAN I HAVE ANY INTEREST IN GOING.
WHO SAID YOU'D BE COMING?
DID I MISS SOMETHING?
WE NEED YOUR SHIP. NOT YOU. LIKE I SAID, IT WOULD BE A SHORT--
NO.
NEVER GONNA HAPPEN.
NO ONE PILOTS THE FALCON BUT ME AND CHEWIE.
HER HIGHNESS HAS LOST IT. WHAT MAKES HER THINK I'D LET ANYONE TAKE MY SHIP FOR ANY REASON?
BECAUSE UNLIKE YOU, OUR LOYALTIES AREN'T CONFLICTED.
WE HELP THE REBELLION WHEN WE CAN. WE'RE TRUSTED.
IN OTHER WORDS, WE'RE LOYAL.
HEY! DID EITHER OF YOU FIGHT IN THE BATTLE OF YAVIN? I HAD A CHANCE TO LEAVE, BUT I CAME BACK--RISKED MY LIFE. IF THAT'S NOT LOYALTY, I DON'T KNOW WHAT IS.
WILL YOU LOAN US THE FALCON OR NOT?
WE WON'T FORCE YOU. BUT WE NEED TO KNOW.
DOESN'T SEEM AS IF YOU'RE DOING ANYTHING ELSE WITH YOUR SHIP RIGHT NOW.
RRRAAAARGH!
IT'S THE TRUTH, CHEWBACCA.

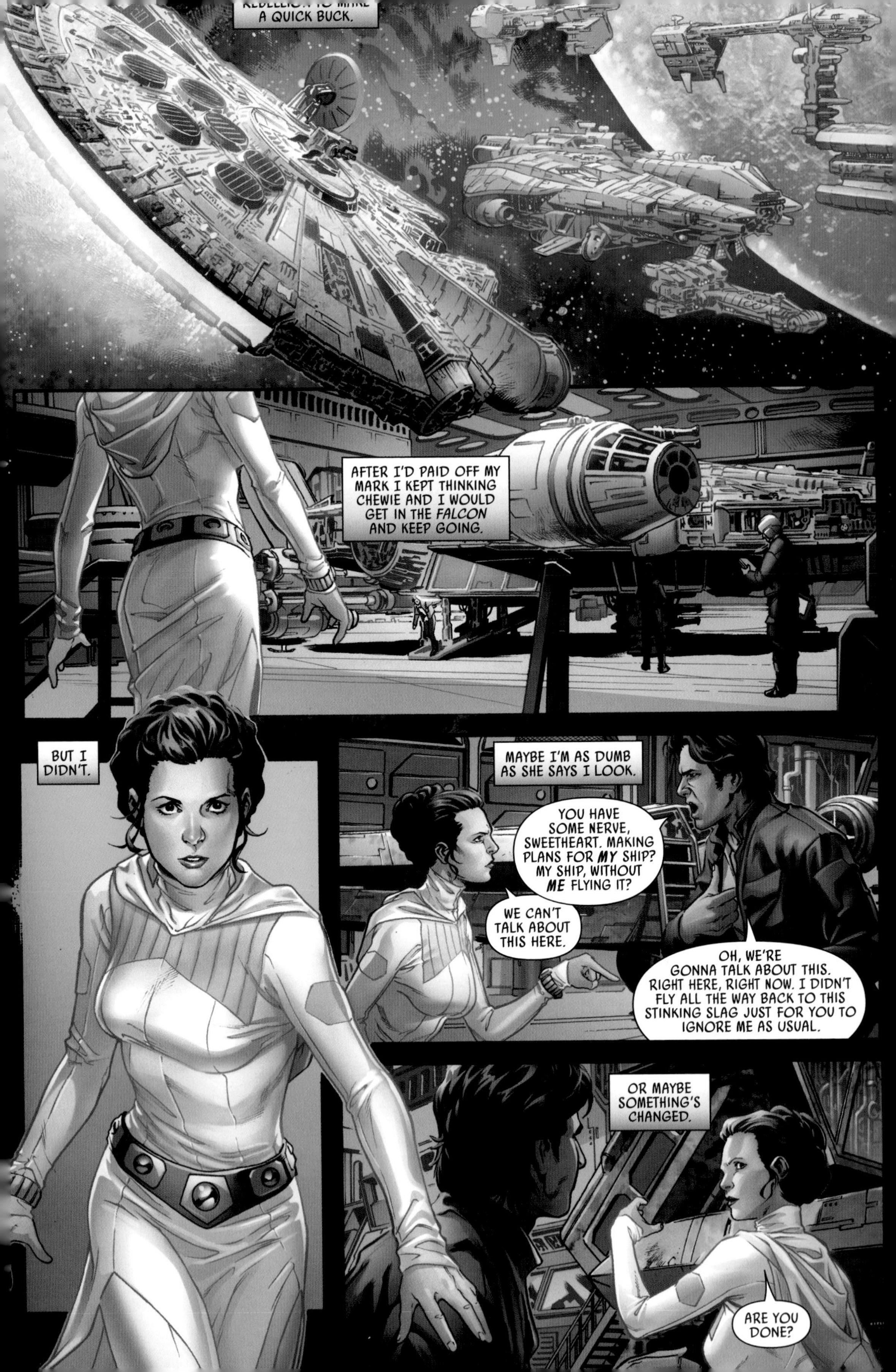
A QUICK BUCK.
AFTER I'D PAID OFF MY MARK I KEPT THINKING CHEWIE AND I WOULD GET IN THE *FALCON* AND KEEP GOING.
BUT I DIDN'T.
MAYBE I'M AS DUMB AS SHE SAYS I LOOK.
YOU HAVE SOME NERVE, SWEETHEART. MAKING PLANS FOR **MY** SHIP? MY SHIP, WITHOUT **ME** FLYING IT?
WE CAN'T TALK ABOUT THIS HERE.
OH, WE'RE GONNA TALK ABOUT THIS. RIGHT HERE, RIGHT NOW. I DIDN'T FLY ALL THE WAY BACK TO THIS STINKING SLAG JUST FOR YOU TO IGNORE ME AS USUAL.
OR MAYBE SOMETHING'S CHANGED.
ARE YOU DONE?

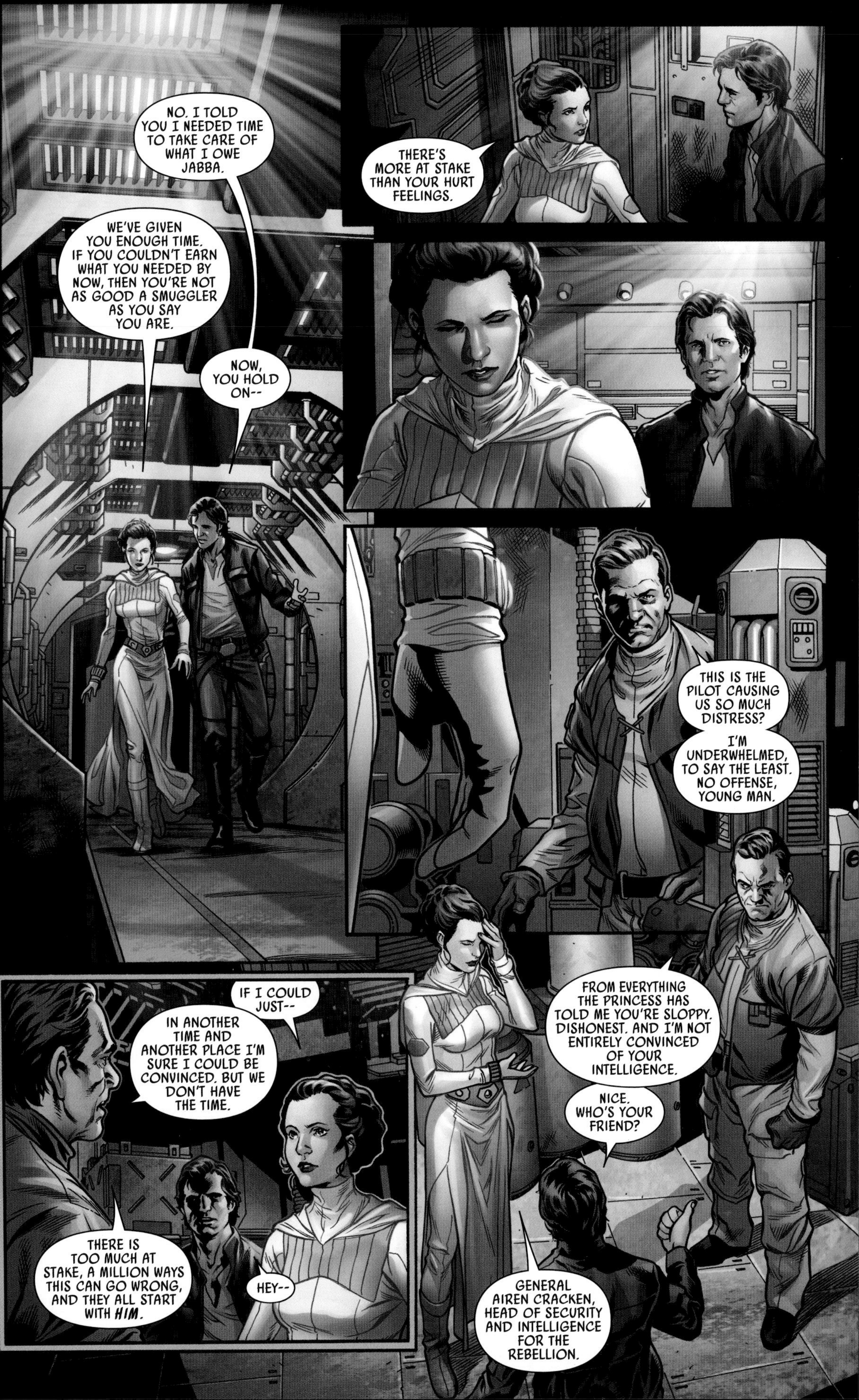
NO. I TOLD YOU I NEEDED TIME TO TAKE CARE OF WHAT I OWE JABBA.
WE'VE GIVEN YOU ENOUGH TIME. IF YOU COULDN'T EARN WHAT YOU NEEDED BY NOW, THEN YOU'RE NOT AS GOOD A SMUGGLER AS YOU SAY YOU ARE.
NOW, YOU HOLD ON--
THERE'S MORE AT STAKE THAN YOUR HURT FEELINGS.
THIS IS THE PILOT CAUSING US SO MUCH DISTRESS?
I'M UNDERWHELMED, TO SAY THE LEAST. NO OFFENSE, YOUNG MAN.
FROM EVERYTHING THE PRINCESS HAS TOLD ME YOU'RE SLOPPY. DISHONEST. AND I'M NOT ENTIRELY CONVINCED OF YOUR INTELLIGENCE.
NICE. WHO'S YOUR FRIEND?
GENERAL AIREN CRACKEN, HEAD OF SECURITY AND INTELLIGENCE FOR THE REBELLION.
IF I COULD JUST--
IN ANOTHER TIME AND ANOTHER PLACE I'M SURE I COULD BE CONVINCED. BUT WE DON'T HAVE THE TIME.
THERE IS TOO MUCH AT STAKE, A MILLION WAYS THIS CAN GO WRONG, AND THEY ALL START WITH *HIM*.
HEY--

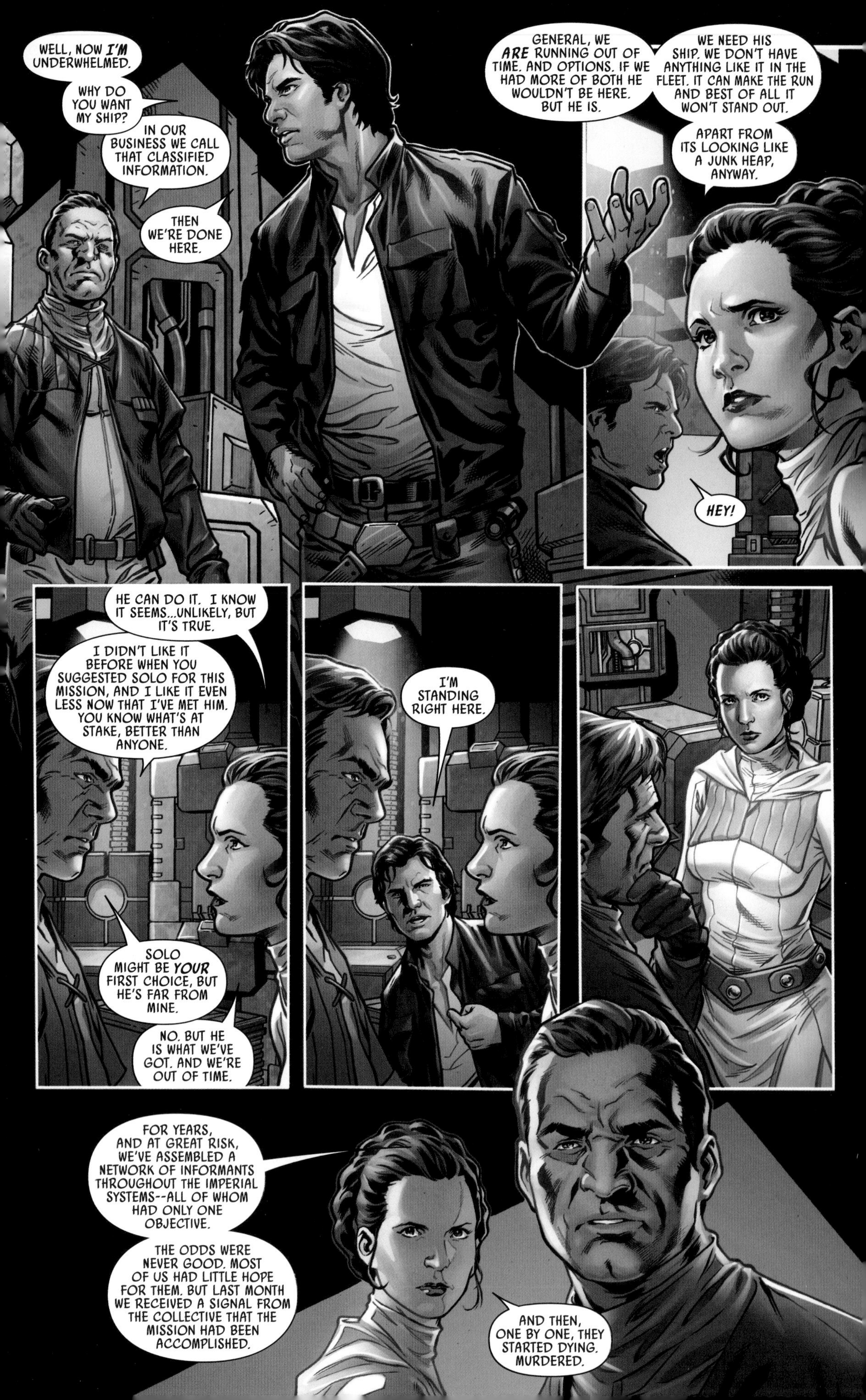
WELL, NOW I'M UNDERWHELMED.
WHY DO YOU WANT MY SHIP?
IN OUR BUSINESS WE CALL THAT CLASSIFIED INFORMATION.
THEN WE'RE DONE HERE.
GENERAL, WE ARE RUNNING OUT OF TIME. AND OPTIONS. IF WE HAD MORE OF BOTH HE WOULDN'T BE HERE. BUT HE IS.
WE NEED HIS SHIP. WE DON'T HAVE ANYTHING LIKE IT IN THE FLEET. IT CAN MAKE THE RUN AND BEST OF ALL IT WON'T STAND OUT.
APART FROM ITS LOOKING LIKE A JUNK HEAP, ANYWAY.
HEY!
HE CAN DO IT. I KNOW IT SEEMS...UNLIKELY, BUT IT'S TRUE.
I DIDN'T LIKE IT BEFORE WHEN YOU SUGGESTED SOLO FOR THIS MISSION, AND I LIKE IT EVEN LESS NOW THAT I'VE MET HIM. YOU KNOW WHAT'S AT STAKE, BETTER THAN ANYONE.
SOLO MIGHT BE YOUR FIRST CHOICE, BUT HE'S FAR FROM MINE.
NO. BUT HE IS WHAT WE'VE GOT. AND WE'RE OUT OF TIME.
I'M STANDING RIGHT HERE.
FOR YEARS, AND AT GREAT RISK, WE'VE ASSEMBLED A NETWORK OF INFORMANTS THROUGHOUT THE IMPERIAL SYSTEMS--ALL OF WHOM HAD ONLY ONE OBJECTIVE.
THE ODDS WERE NEVER GOOD. MOST OF US HAD LITTLE HOPE FOR THEM. BUT LAST MONTH WE RECEIVED A SIGNAL FROM THE COLLECTIVE THAT THE MISSION HAD BEEN ACCOMPLISHED.
AND THEN, ONE BY ONE, THEY STARTED DYING. MURDERED.

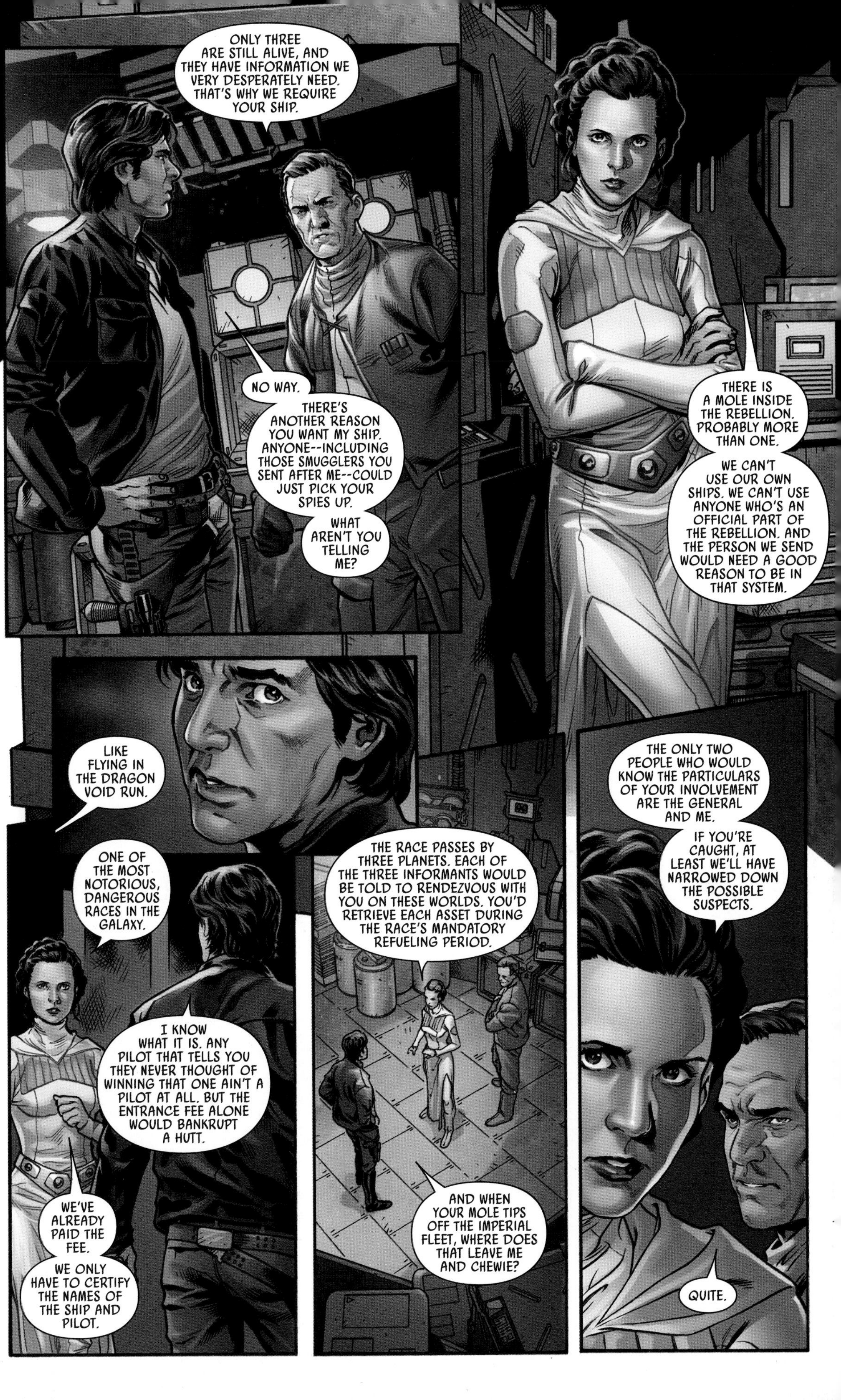
ONLY THREE ARE STILL ALIVE, AND THEY HAVE INFORMATION WE VERY DESPERATELY NEED. THAT'S WHY WE REQUIRE YOUR SHIP.
NO WAY.
THERE'S ANOTHER REASON YOU WANT MY SHIP. ANYONE--INCLUDING THOSE SMUGGLERS YOU SENT AFTER ME--COULD JUST PICK YOUR SPIES UP.
WHAT AREN'T YOU TELLING ME?
THERE IS A MOLE INSIDE THE REBELLION. PROBABLY MORE THAN ONE.
WE CAN'T USE OUR OWN SHIPS. WE CAN'T USE ANYONE WHO'S AN OFFICIAL PART OF THE REBELLION. AND THE PERSON WE SEND WOULD NEED A GOOD REASON TO BE IN THAT SYSTEM.
LIKE FLYING IN THE DRAGON VOID RUN.
ONE OF THE MOST NOTORIOUS, DANGEROUS RACES IN THE GALAXY.
I KNOW WHAT IT IS. ANY PILOT THAT TELLS YOU THEY NEVER THOUGHT OF WINNING THAT ONE AIN'T A PILOT AT ALL. BUT THE ENTRANCE FEE ALONE WOULD BANKRUPT A HUTT.
WE'VE ALREADY PAID THE FEE.
WE ONLY HAVE TO CERTIFY THE NAMES OF THE SHIP AND PILOT.
THE RACE PASSES BY THREE PLANETS. EACH OF THE THREE INFORMANTS WOULD BE TOLD TO RENDEZVOUS WITH YOU ON THESE WORLDS. YOU'D RETRIEVE EACH ASSET DURING THE RACE'S MANDATORY REFUELING PERIOD.
AND WHEN YOUR MOLE TIPS OFF THE IMPERIAL FLEET, WHERE DOES THAT LEAVE ME AND CHEWIE?
THE ONLY TWO PEOPLE WHO WOULD KNOW THE PARTICULARS OF YOUR INVOLVEMENT ARE THE GENERAL AND ME.
IF YOU'RE CAUGHT, AT LEAST WE'LL HAVE NARROWED DOWN THE POSSIBLE SUSPECTS.
QUITE.

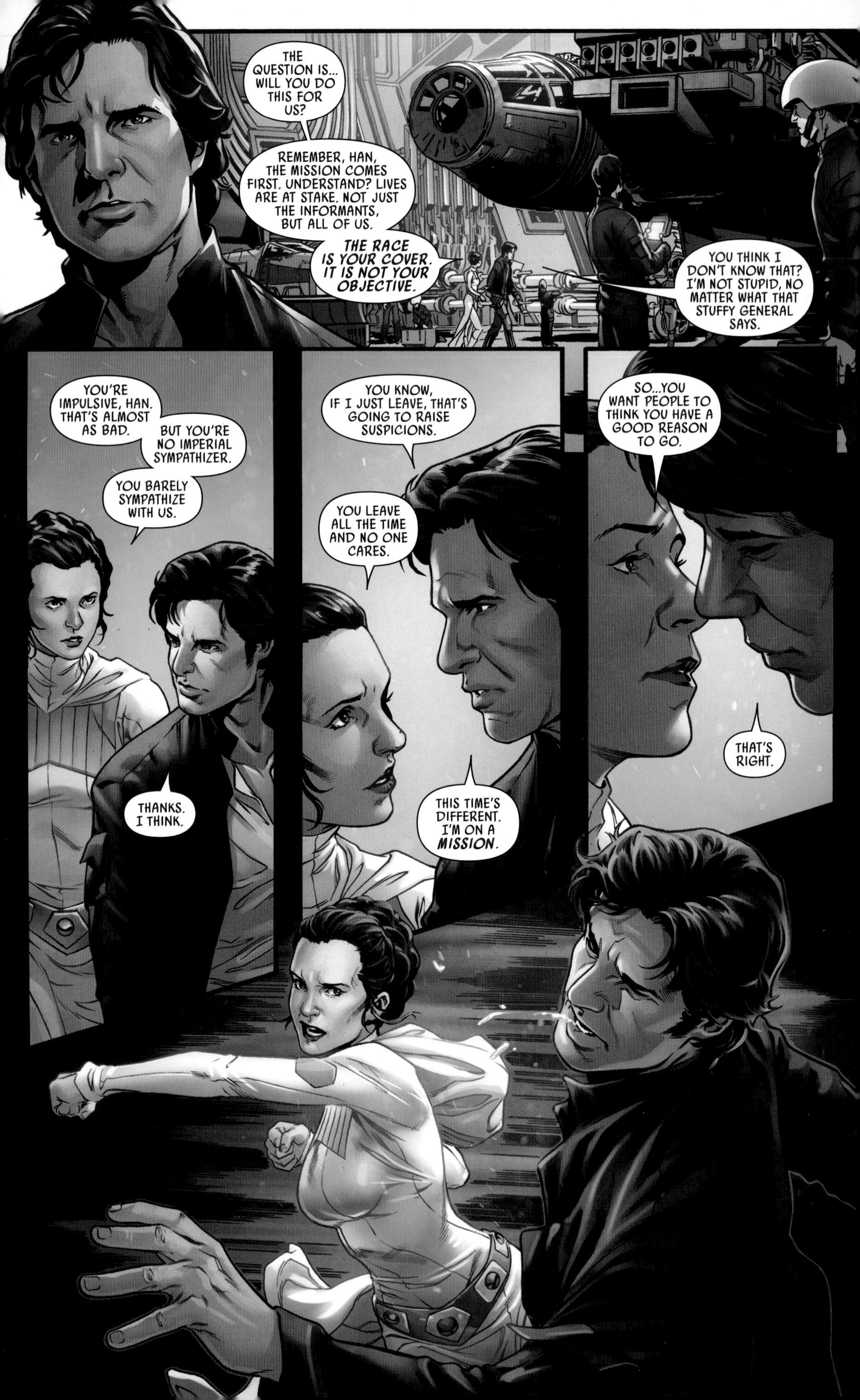
THE QUESTION IS... WILL YOU DO THIS FOR US?
REMEMBER, HAN, THE MISSION COMES FIRST. UNDERSTAND? LIVES ARE AT STAKE. NOT JUST THE INFORMANTS, BUT ALL OF US.
THE RACE IS YOUR COVER. IT IS NOT YOUR OBJECTIVE.
YOU THINK I DON'T KNOW THAT? I'M NOT STUPID, NO MATTER WHAT THAT STUFFY GENERAL SAYS.
YOU'RE IMPULSIVE, HAN. THAT'S ALMOST AS BAD.
BUT YOU'RE NO IMPERIAL SYMPATHIZER.
YOU BARELY SYMPATHIZE WITH US.
THANKS. I THINK.
YOU KNOW, IF I JUST LEAVE, THAT'S GOING TO RAISE SUSPICIONS.
YOU LEAVE ALL THE TIME AND NO ONE CARES.
THIS TIME'S DIFFERENT. I'M ON A MISSION.
SO...YOU WANT PEOPLE TO THINK YOU HAVE A GOOD REASON TO GO.
THAT'S RIGHT.

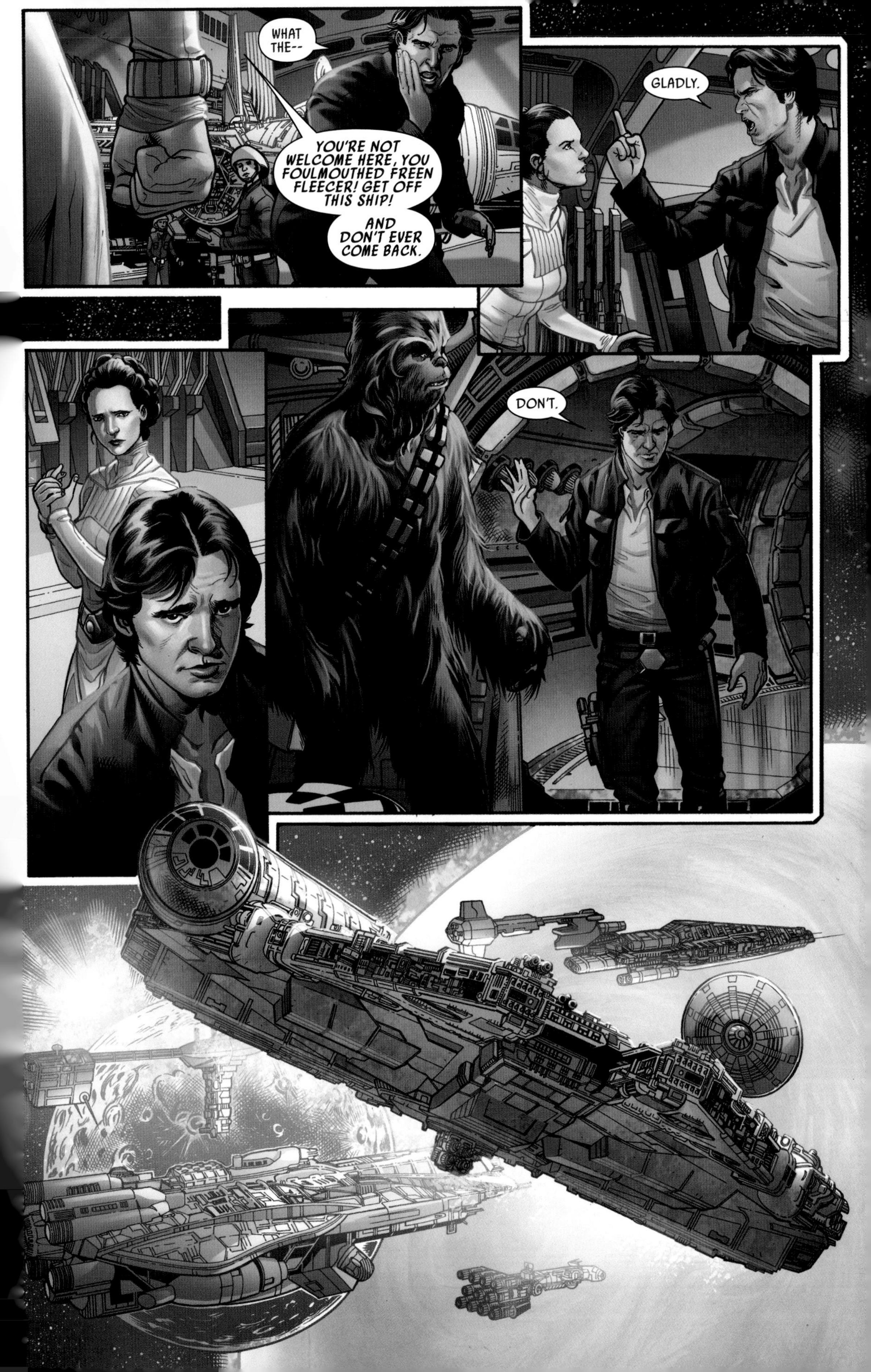
WHAT THE--
YOU'RE NOT WELCOME HERE, YOU FOULMOUTHED FREEN FLEECER! GET OFF THIS SHIP!
AND DON'T EVER COME BACK.
GLADLY.
DON'T.

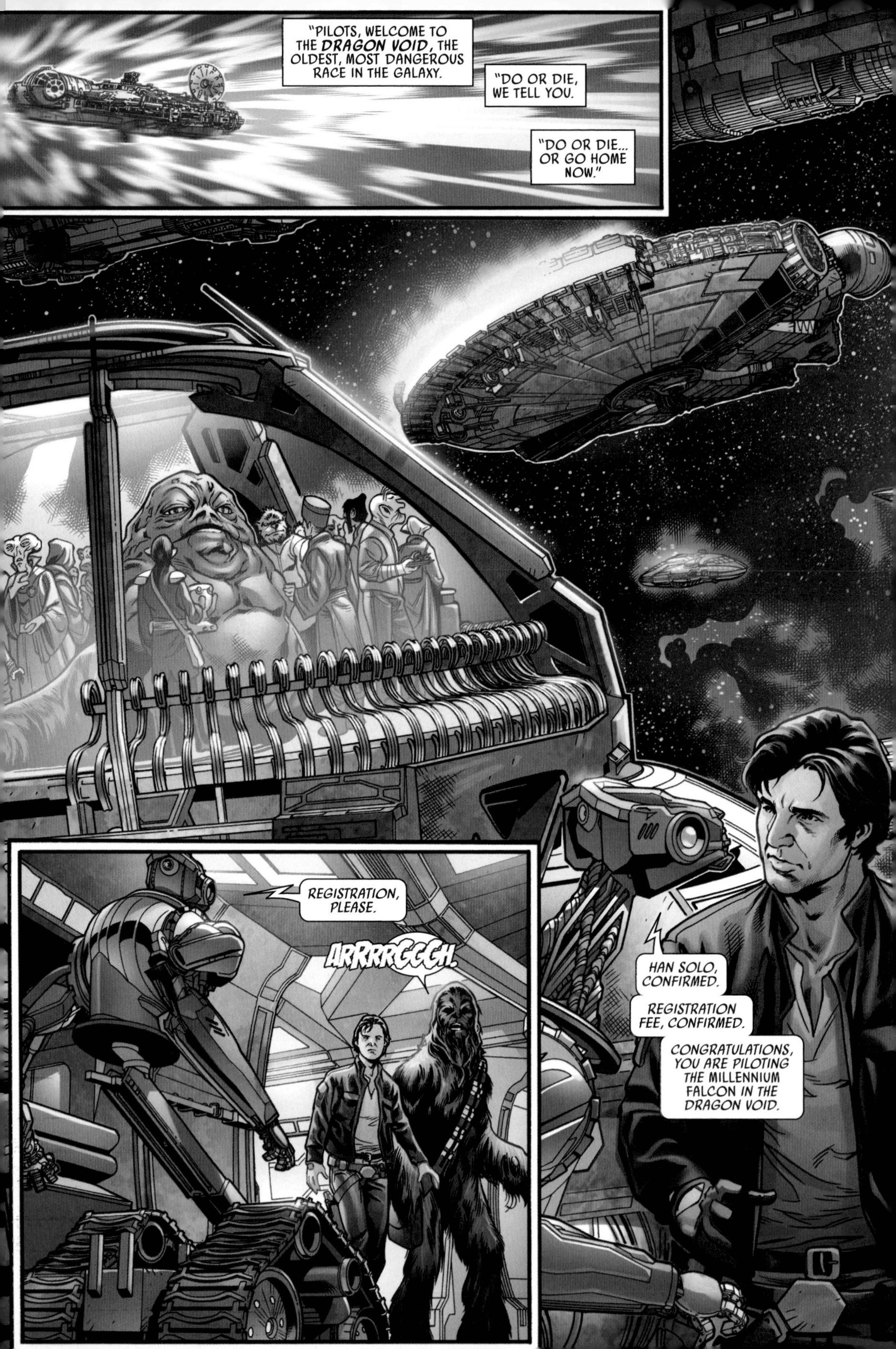
"PILOTS, WELCOME TO THE DRAGON VOID, THE OLDEST, MOST DANGEROUS RACE IN THE GALAXY.
"DO OR DIE, WE TELL YOU.
"DO OR DIE... OR GO HOME NOW."
REGISTRATION, PLEASE.
ARRRRGGGH.
HAN SOLO, CONFIRMED.
REGISTRATION FEE, CONFIRMED.
CONGRATULATIONS, YOU ARE PILOTING THE MILLENNIUM FALCON IN THE DRAGON VOID.

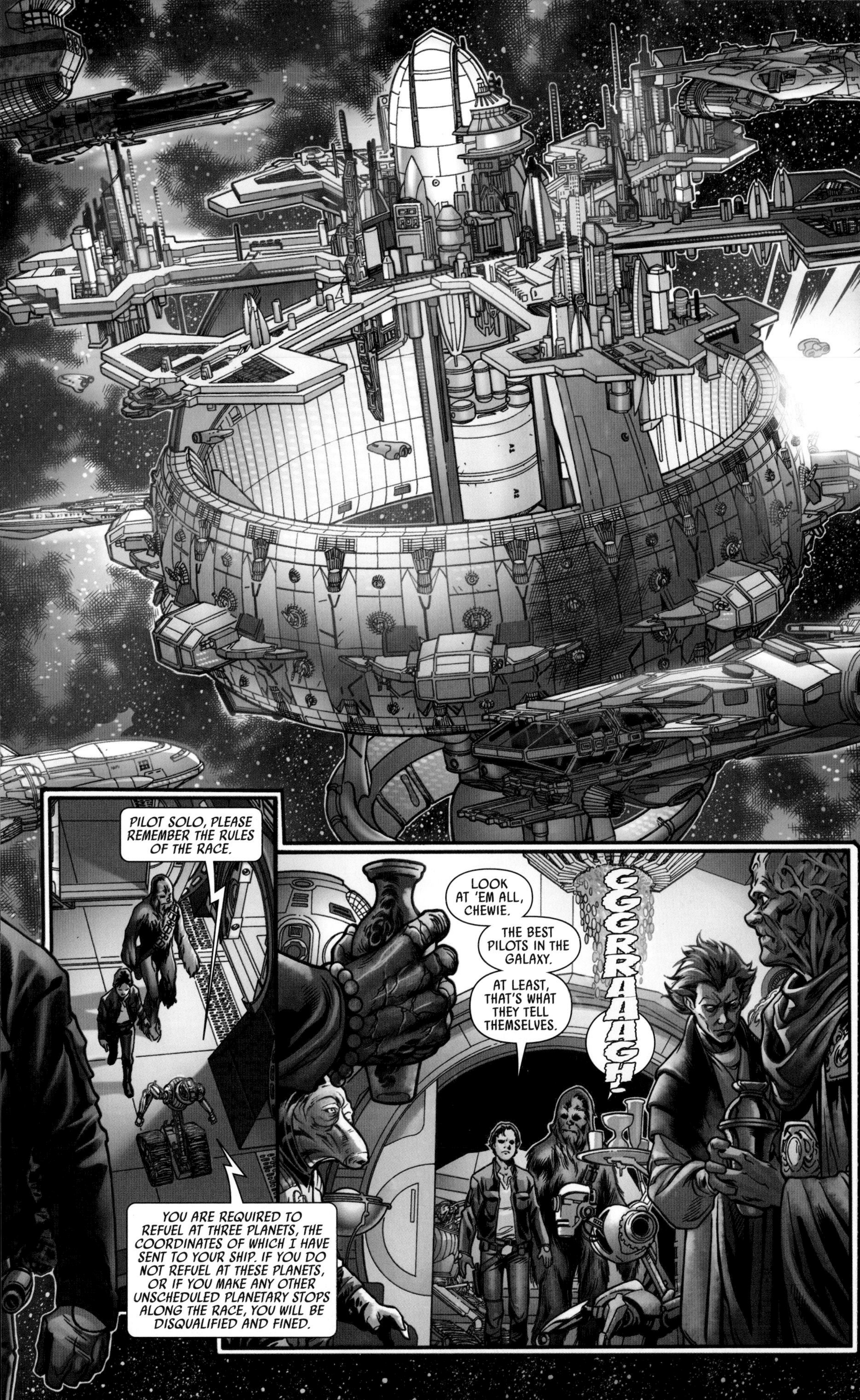
PILOT SOLO, PLEASE REMEMBER THE RULES OF THE RACE.
YOU ARE REQUIRED TO REFUEL AT THREE PLANETS, THE COORDINATES OF WHICH I HAVE SENT TO YOUR SHIP. IF YOU DO NOT REFUEL AT THESE PLANETS, OR IF YOU MAKE ANY OTHER UNSCHEDULED PLANETARY STOPS ALONG THE RACE, YOU WILL BE DISQUALIFIED AND FINED.
LOOK AT 'EM ALL, CHEWIE.
THE BEST PILOTS IN THE GALAXY.
AT LEAST, THAT'S WHAT THEY TELL THEMSELVES.
GGGRRAAAAGH!

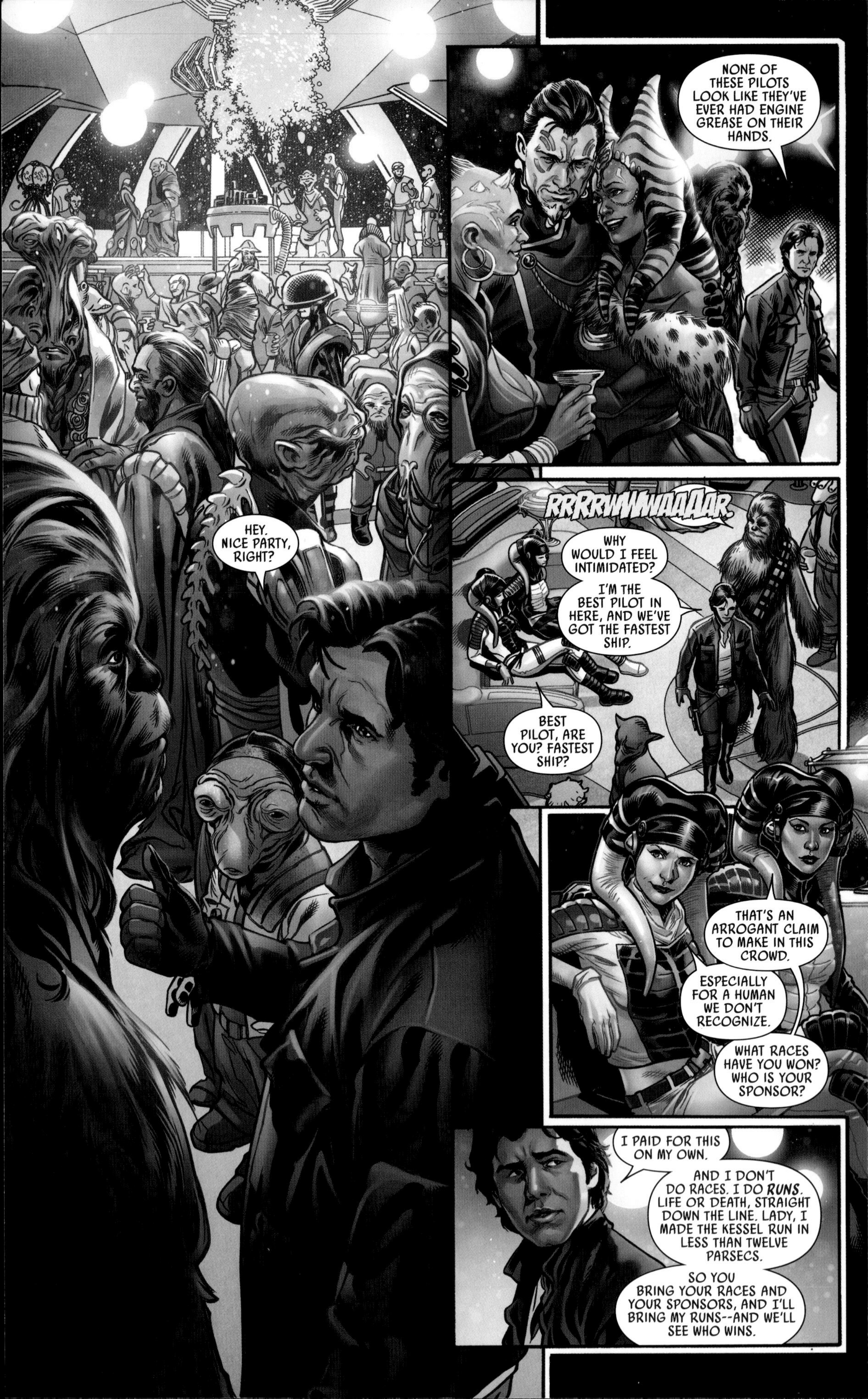
HEY. NICE PARTY, RIGHT?
NONE OF THESE PILOTS LOOK LIKE THEY'VE EVER HAD ENGINE GREASE ON THEIR HANDS.
RRRRWWWAAAAR.
WHY WOULD I FEEL INTIMIDATED?
I'M THE BEST PILOT IN HERE, AND WE'VE GOT THE FASTEST SHIP.
BEST PILOT, ARE YOU? FASTEST SHIP?
THAT'S AN ARROGANT CLAIM TO MAKE IN THIS CROWD.
ESPECIALLY FOR A HUMAN WE DON'T RECOGNIZE.
WHAT RACES HAVE YOU WON? WHO IS YOUR SPONSOR?
I PAID FOR THIS ON MY OWN.
AND I DON'T DO RACES. I DO *RUNS*. LIFE OR DEATH, STRAIGHT DOWN THE LINE. LADY, I MADE THE KESSEL RUN IN LESS THAN TWELVE PARSECS.
SO YOU BRING YOUR RACES AND YOUR SPONSORS, AND I'LL BRING MY RUNS--AND WE'LL SEE WHO WINS.

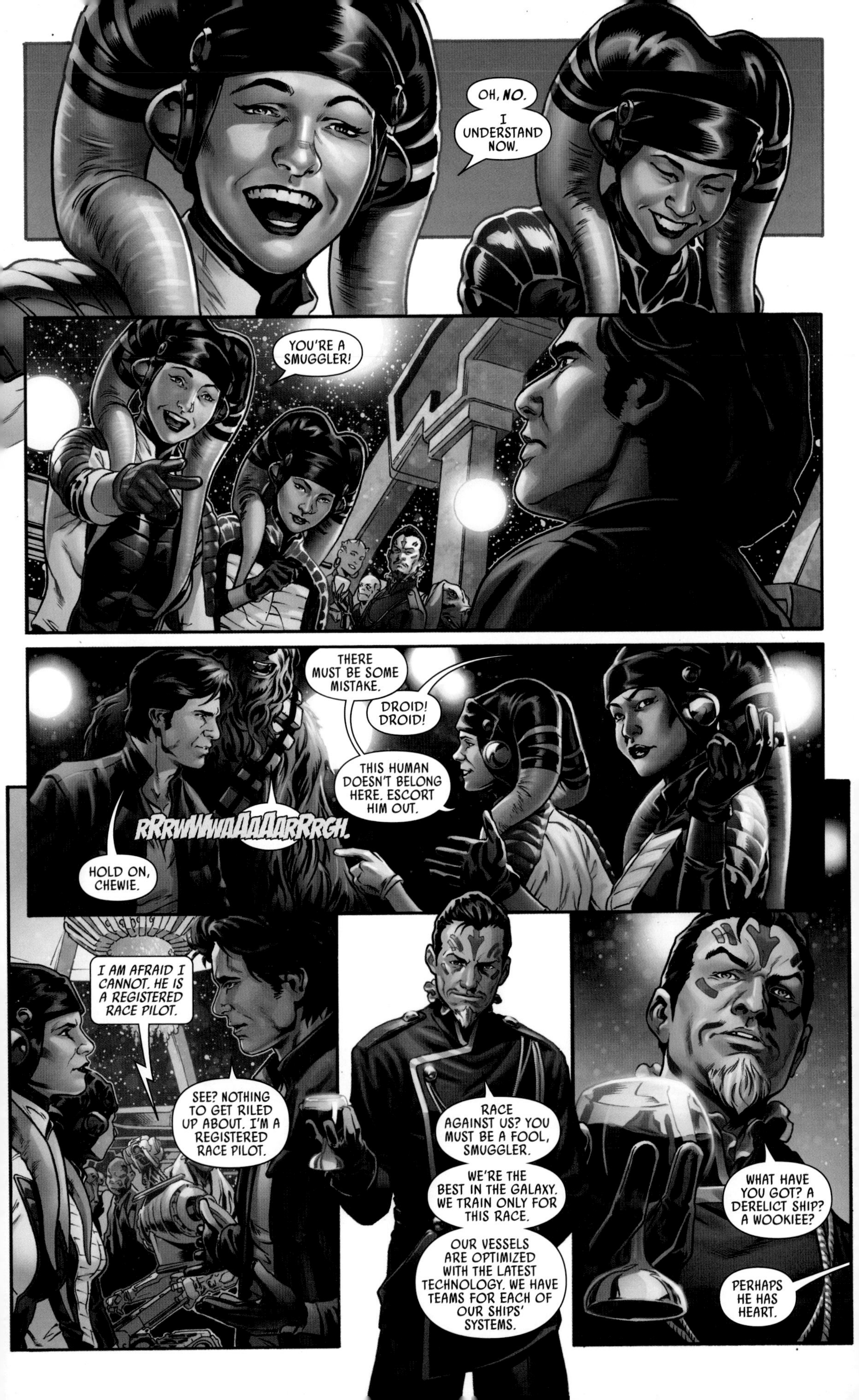
OH, NO.
I UNDERSTAND NOW.
YOU'RE A SMUGGLER!
THERE MUST BE SOME MISTAKE.
DROID! DROID!
THIS HUMAN DOESN'T BELONG HERE. ESCORT HIM OUT.
RRRWWWWAAAAARRRGH.
HOLD ON, CHEWIE.
I AM AFRAID I CANNOT. HE IS A REGISTERED RACE PILOT.
SEE? NOTHING TO GET RILED UP ABOUT. I'M A REGISTERED RACE PILOT.
RACE AGAINST US? YOU MUST BE A FOOL, SMUGGLER.
WE'RE THE BEST IN THE GALAXY. WE TRAIN ONLY FOR THIS RACE.
OUR VESSELS ARE OPTIMIZED WITH THE LATEST TECHNOLOGY. WE HAVE TEAMS FOR EACH OF OUR SHIPS' SYSTEMS.
WHAT HAVE YOU GOT? A DERELICT SHIP? A WOOKIEE?
PERHAPS HE HAS HEART.

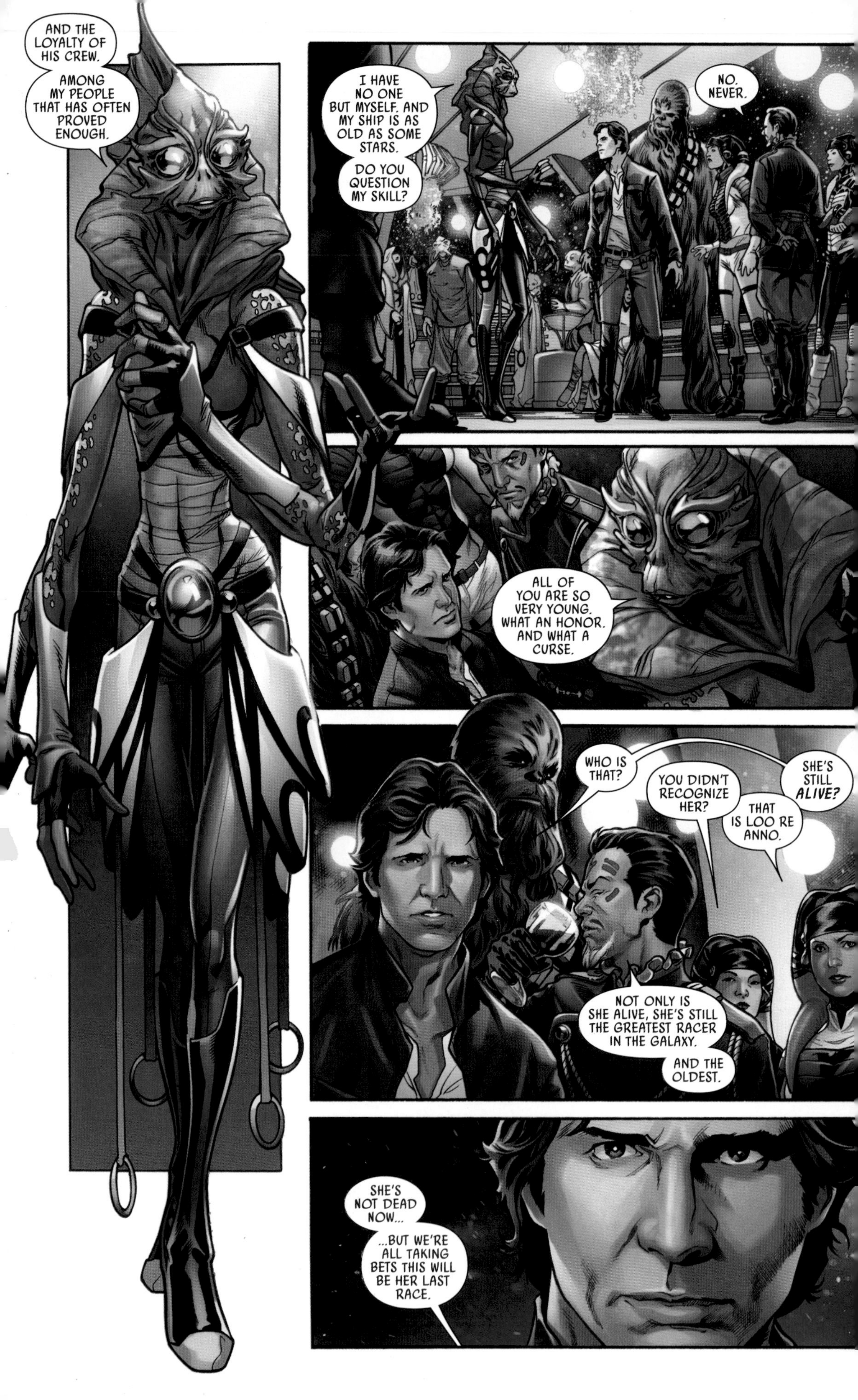
AND THE LOYALTY OF HIS CREW.
AMONG MY PEOPLE THAT HAS OFTEN PROVED ENOUGH.
I HAVE NO ONE BUT MYSELF. AND MY SHIP IS AS OLD AS SOME STARS.
DO YOU QUESTION MY SKILL?
NO. NEVER.
ALL OF YOU ARE SO VERY YOUNG. WHAT AN HONOR. AND WHAT A CURSE.
WHO IS THAT?
YOU DIDN'T RECOGNIZE HER?
SHE'S STILL *ALIVE?*
THAT IS LOO RE ANNO.
NOT ONLY IS SHE ALIVE, SHE'S STILL THE GREATEST RACER IN THE GALAXY.
AND THE OLDEST.
SHE'S NOT DEAD NOW...
...BUT WE'RE ALL TAKING BETS THIS WILL BE HER LAST RACE.

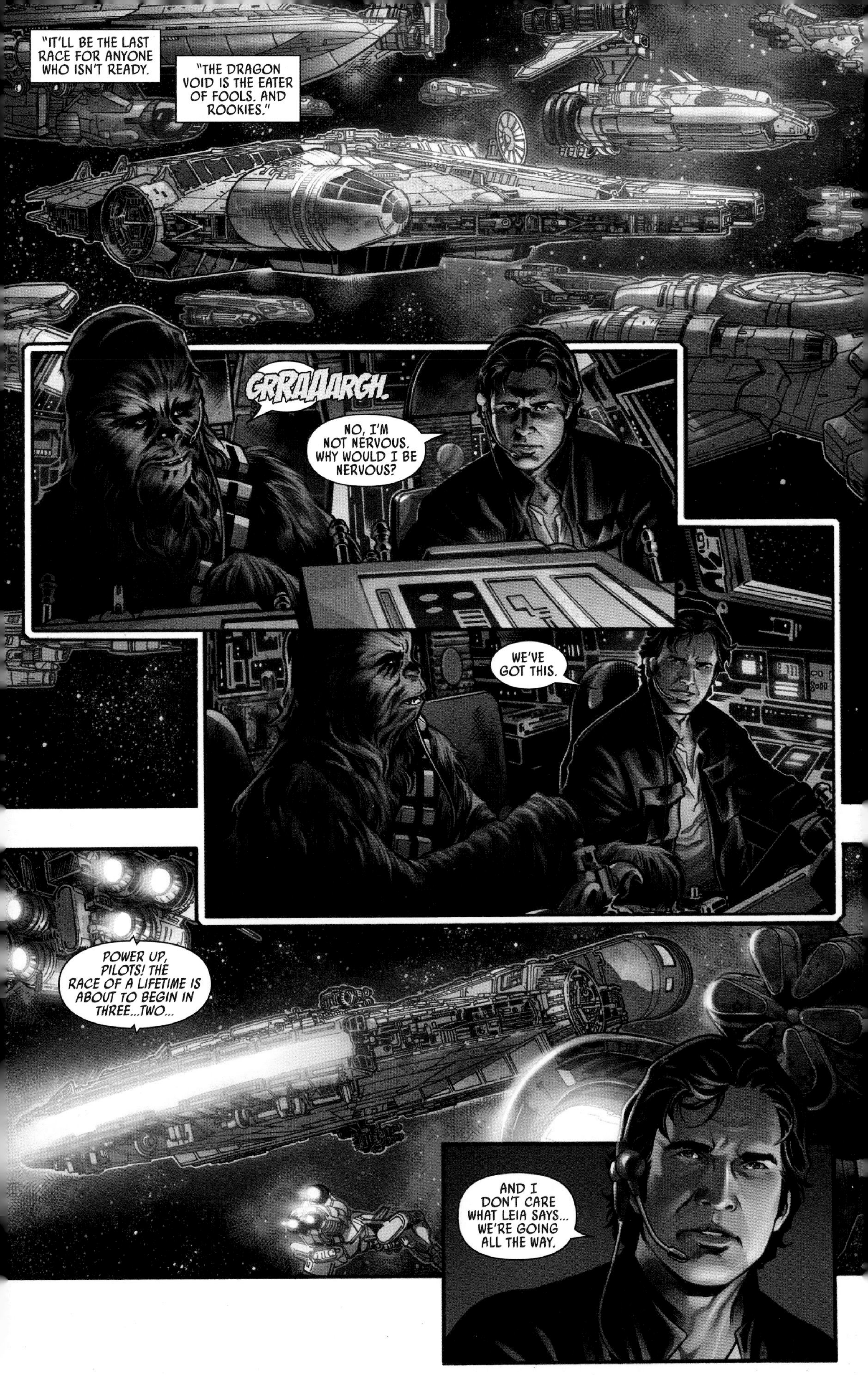

"IT'LL BE THE LAST RACE FOR ANYONE WHO ISN'T READY.
"THE DRAGON VOID IS THE EATER OF FOOLS. AND ROOKIES."
GRRAAARGH.
NO, I'M NOT NERVOUS. WHY WOULD I BE NERVOUS?
WE'VE GOT THIS.
POWER UP, PILOTS! THE RACE OF A LIFETIME IS ABOUT TO BEGIN IN THREE...TWO...
AND I DON'T CARE WHAT LEIA SAYS... WE'RE GOING ALL THE WAY.

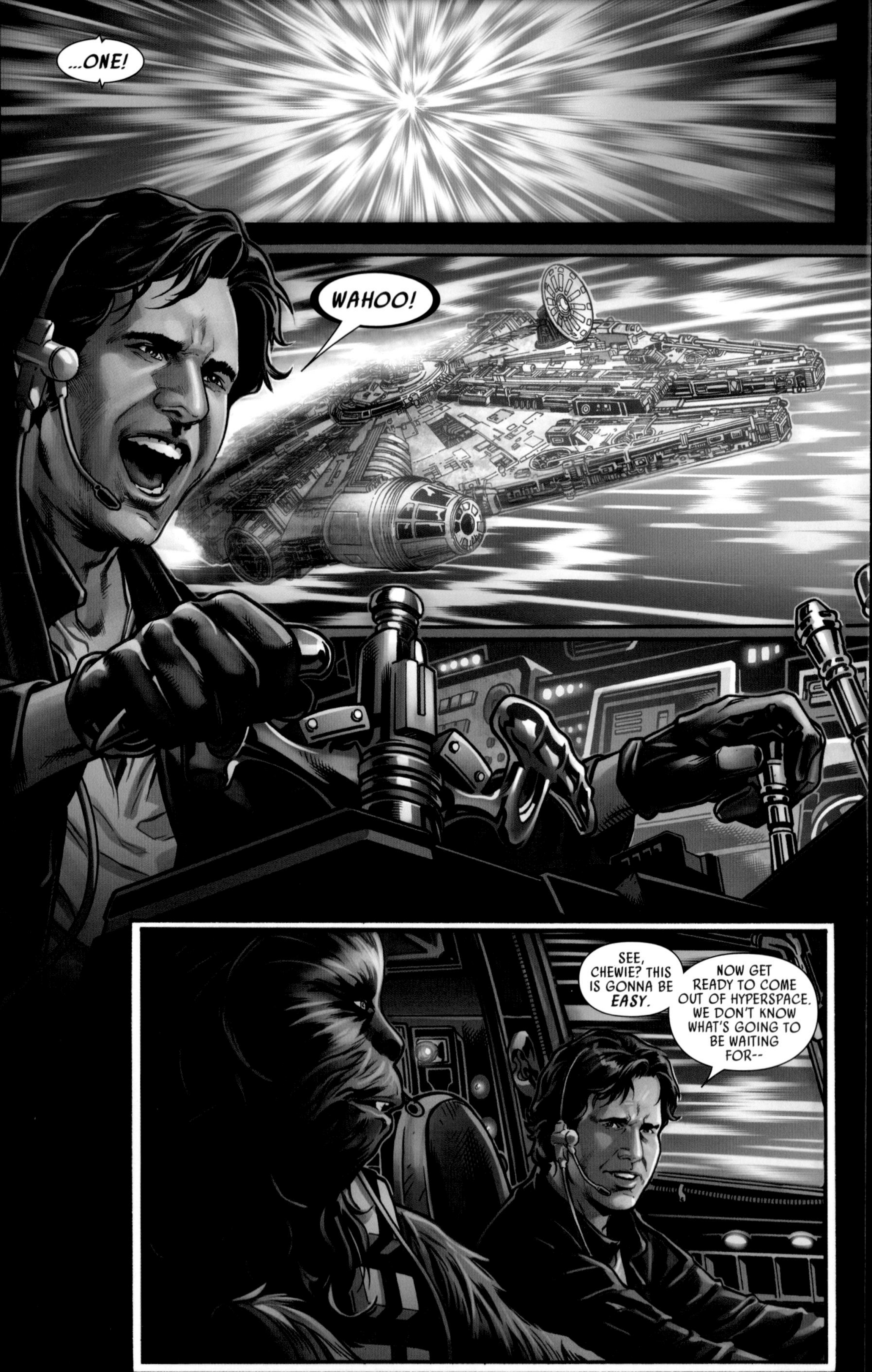
...ONE!
WAHOO!
SEE, CHEWIE? THIS IS GONNA BE EASY.
NOW GET READY TO COME OUT OF HYPERSPACE. WE DON'T KNOW WHAT'S GOING TO BE WAITING FOR--

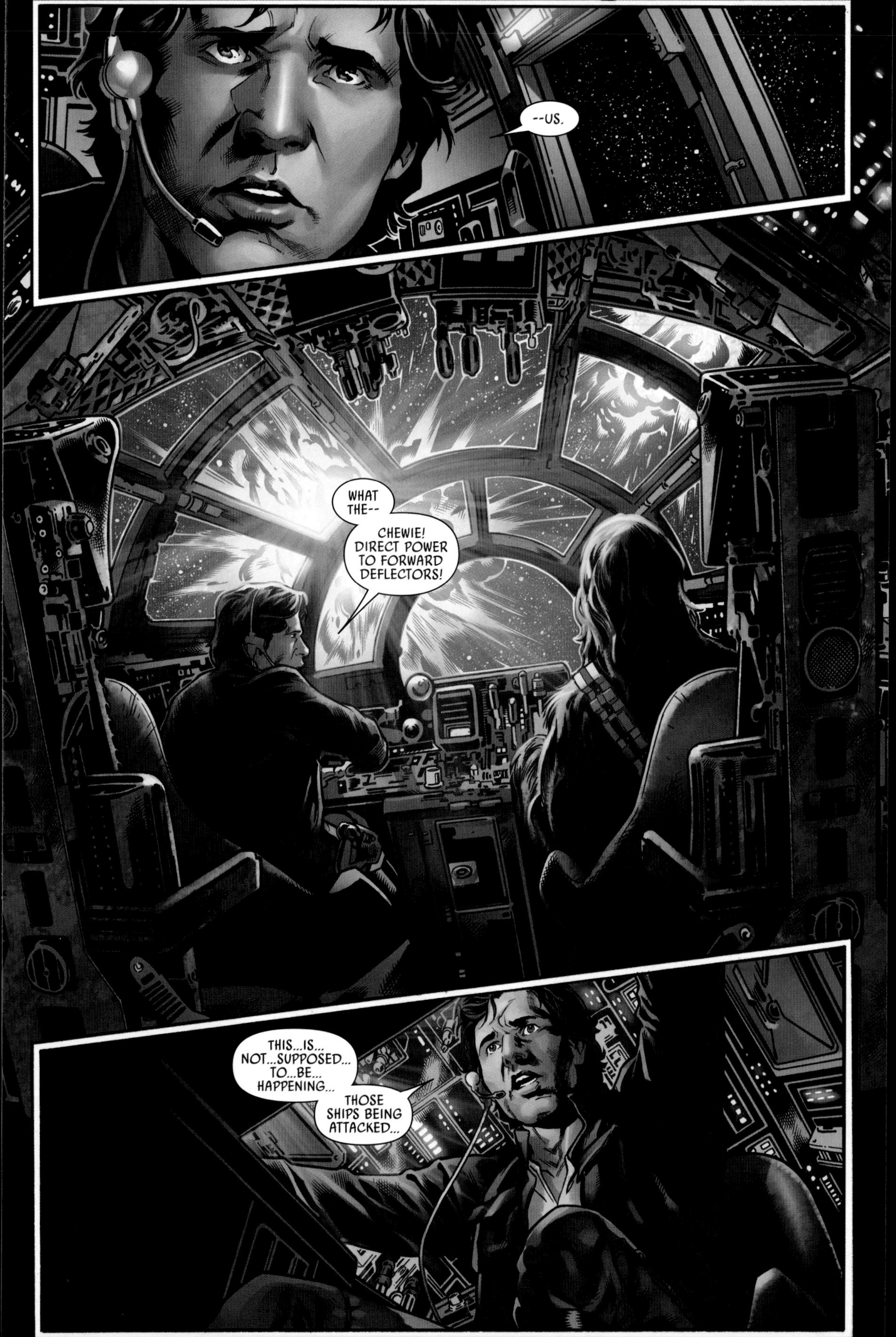
--US.
WHAT THE--
CHEWIE! DIRECT POWER TO FORWARD DEFLECTORS!
THIS...IS... NOT...SUPPOSED... TO...BE... HAPPENING...
THOSE SHIPS BEING ATTACKED...

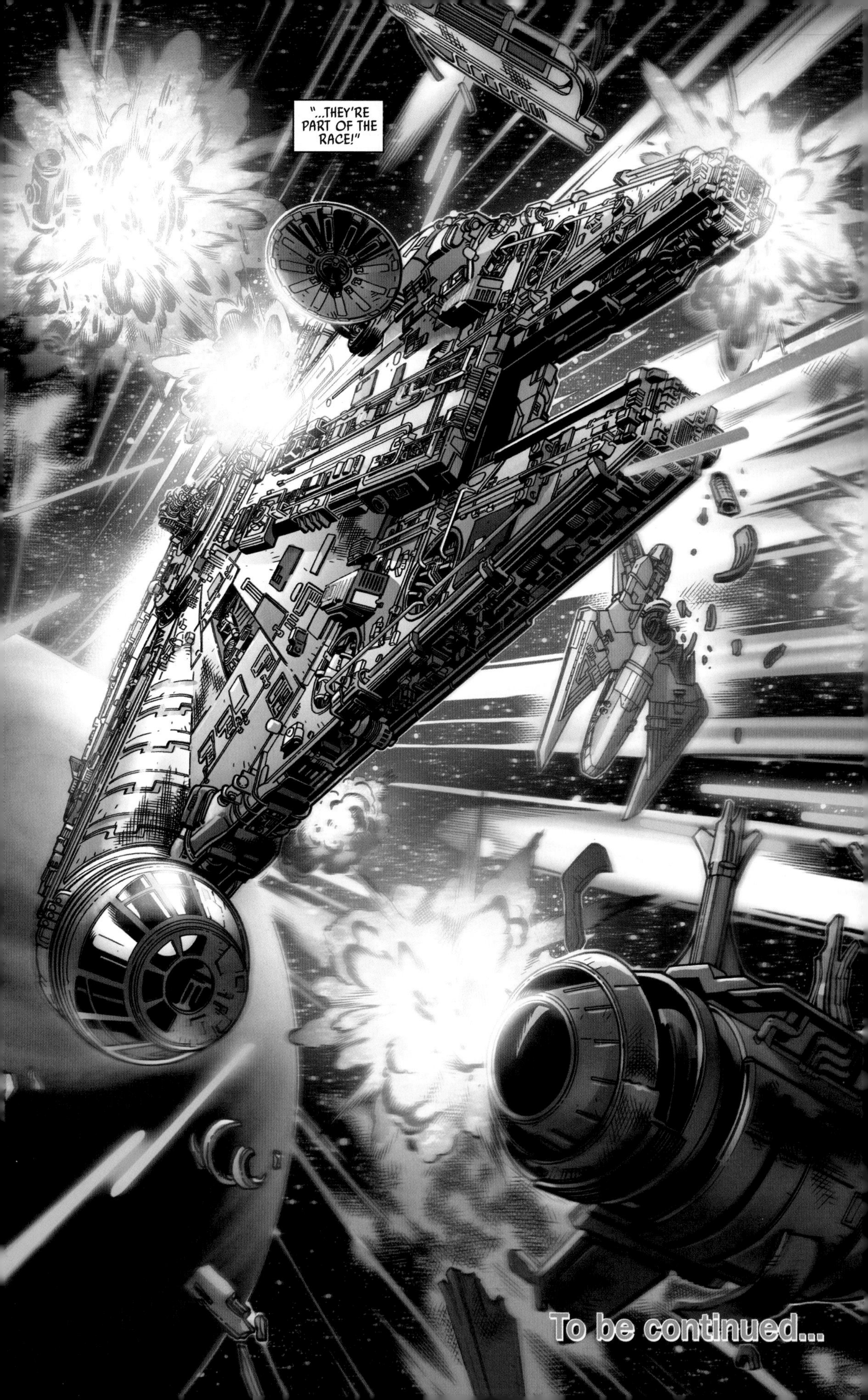
"...THEY'RE PART OF THE RACE!"
To be continued...

STAR WARS™

HAN SOLO

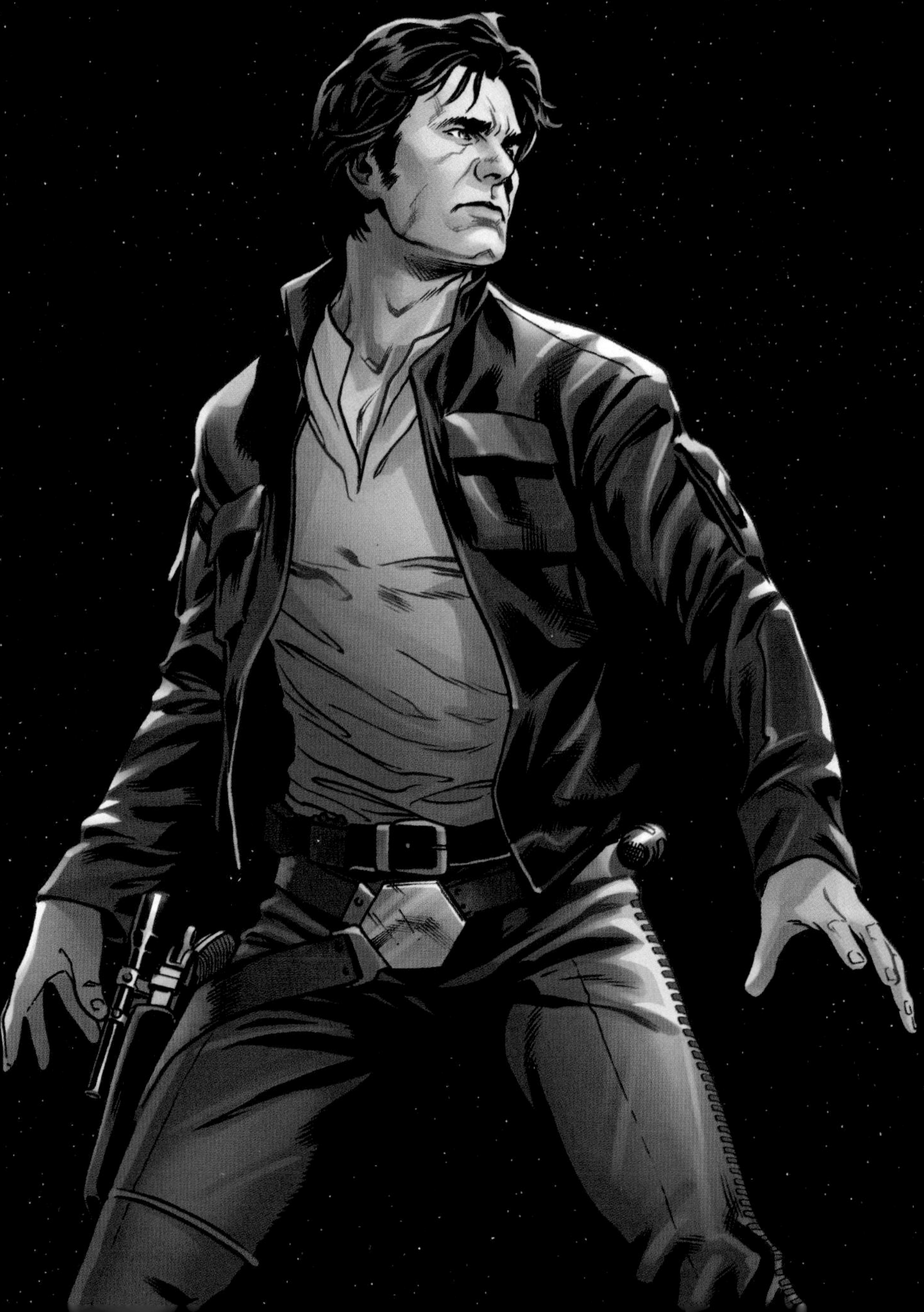

STAR WARS

HAN SOLO

COLLECT THEM ALL!

Set of 5 Hardcover Books ISBN: 978-1-5321-4014-3

STAR WARS
STAR WARS
HAN SOLO
HAN SOLO: VOLUME 1
LIU BROOKS OBACK

Hardcover Book ISBN
978-1-5321-4015-0

STAR WARS
STAR WARS
HAN SOLO
HAN SOLO: VOLUME 2
LIU BROOKS OBACK

Hardcover Book ISBN
978-1-5321-4016-7

STAR WARS
STAR WARS
HAN SOLO
HAN SOLO: VOLUME 3
LIU BROOKS OBACK

Hardcover Book ISBN
978-1-5321-4017-4

STAR WARS
STAR WARS
HAN SOLO
HAN SOLO: VOLUME 4
LIU BROOKS OBACK MILLA

Hardcover Book ISBN
978-1-5321-4018-1

STAR WARS
STAR WARS
HAN SOLO
HAN SOLO: VOLUME 5
LIU BROOKS OBACK

Hardcover Book ISBN
978-1-5321-4019-8

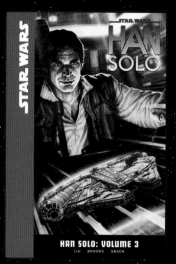

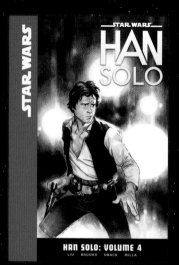